Boxer

Earns His Wings

Douglas Van Dyke Jr.

Boxer
Earns His Wings

This is a work of fiction. Names, characters, places, and events are either the product of the author's imagination or used fictitiously. The world herein described is an alternate-Earth setting. While it may share similarities to our world, and modified names of real-Earth locations, the author maintained a unique setting with public domain or self-created properties.

This edition published through Ingram

ISBN: 978-1-949060-02-7
BISAC FIC002000 Fiction Action & Adventure
       FIC028060 Fiction/SciFict/Steampunk
       FIC004000 Fiction Alternate History

PUBLISHED BY Douglas Van Dyke Jr
Please Visit:
http://dhealoral.com

Retail Price: $10.00

Preview

I hang off the bottom of the airplane, offering me a nice view of the two bombs. The train cars rumble right below, though Dame's trying to line up directly over them. The track has a few curves to it, and sometimes the airplane's momentum has me swinging side to side. Train smoke blows into my face. It seems like it's a short enough fall, but everything's moving out of tandem as I watch car after car pass by. The tankers are left behind and now I'm dangling over boxcars. My arms are straining as I try to time a good jump. No, not yet. Not that one. Maybe, no, I don't like the angle. Shoot, I'm going to run out of cars soon.

Ahead, a hatch pops open atop one of the cars. A figure emerges, looking around. He wears one of those weird leather masks on his head. He's looking the wrong way, but the airplane is coming up on him fast. He'll either see or hear us any moment. I drop my right hand free, reach into my pocket and slip on one of my personalized brass knuckles. He's turning in my direction. I don't like the angle of the jump…

…but then I fall anyway.

Acknowledgments

My biggest appreciation is for my fans who have given me such good reviews and ratings. Whenever I see those good praises and stars on Amazon or Goodreads, it floats my entire day! I'm glad to catch all of you that met me at the local conventions and took a chance on an indy author. Also, thanks for your encouragement on my social media! (Listed on the "About the Author" page in the back.)

Thanks to my editor, Denise Guibord, for all her input and catches. It wouldn't be as smooth of a story without her help.

My appreciation to Bobooks for the cover work! Great job and quick service!

And I love my supportive family. Thanks to my wife and children for their patience and assistance with my writing passion.

Boxer Earns His Wings

I'm staring past my raised fists and bloody knuckles at what might as well be my own reflection: a muscular brawler, similarly stripped to the waist, covered in sweat, taking turns spitting gobs of blood. He's even got my dance steps, the only kind I know how to do. It's a dance in which we circle the square ring until one of us ends up kissing the mat for ten seconds. I can see the blood on his knuckles past the loose skin flaps covering my own. No gloves to soften this man's game. We have only a few supportive bandages from fingers down to wrists for when the fist tenderizes the meat. So far, the blood and bruises we've donated have just been us testing each other. Mere foreplay for those witnesses cheering and jeering.

In the darkness surrounding us are a few invested wallets hiding behind loud mouths. Some come in leaving a sod trail, sporting revolvers, and wearing their cowboy hats and spurs. Other rowdies let loose after spending their strenuous day swinging big sledges to connect the railroad across the continent. Most of those strong backs barely have money to spare for gambling, but they laid down the track that brought the rest of the coins here. The most dangerous men in the audience possess neither weapons nor strong arms. They wear tailored suits, the rich fabric boasting of backroom deals over thick cigars and deep pockets for buying anyone and anything in here. Their cologne does little to disguise the tobacco smell. Regardless of scented or sweaty, full pockets or moth-ridden, the roomful of folks sits on the same beer-stained benches as their stomping feet crunch spilled peanuts. Most of the crowd shout a din of instructions. Of course, we ignore them. We're the two alpha males sharing the spotlight. I haven't got a care for any distraction from amateurs who won't ante up their own bodies for the ring.

A door opens and a shaft of light interrupts the tobacco-fog darkness. Two more fine-tailored suits walk into the room. They swagger in with the confidence instilled by their hidden badges, but I know they wear them. Those polished stars are likely pinned next to concealed, government-issued sidearms. These particular suits always bring me trouble.

True to our past interactions, things go south right away. My distraction nearly costs me a tooth as a well-timed hook sneaks by and spins me at the cheek. I'm stumbling backward, trying to re-orient my head. I throw out a jab just in case it gets lucky or slows him. Before I'm properly set, I feel my right arm touch the rope.

I really don't like getting backed into the rope.

We trade a flurry of blows, so close we're almost hugging. Finally, I give him a shove that backs him up and gives me time for a breath. The old routine returns: dancing, sweating, spitting. I cast a glance over to my ringside friend, Jerry. In between taking bets and counting money, he gives me the sign. Apparently, my recent setback against the ropes served some good purpose. It seems enough people still haven't heard about me, so they start betting bet their money to the other guy. They don't know they are giving in to a sure loss. Normally, this is where I begin wearing the other guy down slowly and put him away. Between Jerry and me, we'll take in a nice haul. Unfortunately, my hot temper is boiling over at the appearance of the suits and what they represent. Getting backed against the ropes didn't help my mood either. This guy is about to find out why everywhere I go, everyone calls me 'Boxer,' as if I was the only one.

My jab convinces him to raise his arms higher for a moment. He's distracted as my right uppercut to his abdomen lifts him off the mat. As he drops, his torso and arms plunge too low. A left hook drops the rest of his defenses. My right cross slams his head backward until it bounces off the canvas. The yelling and cursing in the crowd hits a new high. The referee starts counting but I know there's no need. Even Jerry is looking up at me, stunned that I pummeled the guy so quickly. I wasn't showing off for the loud crowd of wallets. My show was aimed at the two badges who will be cornering me when I'm alone.

*   *   *

The proprietor of the place gave me a nice room with a clawfoot tub for cleaning up, as I'd requested earlier in the day. Normally, I like to get clean after a fight, put on an enticing musk scent from a bottle, and dress up as fine as those suits who interrupted the fight. It's not that I prefer fancy clothes, they are more like a costume to me. I guess it's my own little joke to fight dirty and dress dandy. I'm a fan of sarcasm.

Not today. Since I know those government lackeys will be turning up anytime, I change my routine. I start shadow-boxing, push-ups, arm curls—anything to work up even more of a sweat. A bar supporting a divider curtain hangs near the tub, useful for pull-ups. Shirtless, my chest and back display every knife wound, burn scar, and puckered shrapnel entry I've ever earned. On a good note, the doctor's fees from most of those injuries weren't mine to worry about. They just added to the bill for those who kept wrangling me into shit jobs. To add to the intimidation, I even leave my personalized brass knuckles lying nearby, just to complete the image. The only thing not displayed is my six-shooter, since it's often a good idea to keep a hidden ace.

I hear Jerry's voice from the other side of the door. "…not after last time! He came back with three broken ribs, and a warrant for his arrest in Wauthec Springs! He's only just now been able to book fights again…"

Jerry tries hard, but he really is out of his league. Within a couple breaths, the two suits have already pushed through the door and slammed it shut on poor Jerry. I courteously restrict myself to only two more pull-ups while they stand there clearing their throats. As my weight drops from the divider bar, the floor rattles.

"Hello, Pops." I say to the older one. "Hello, Dongel." I call him Dongel because he hates it.

Pops answers, "Those aren't our code names."

"Well, since you won't give me your real names, I'll make up my own nicknames."

It's no secret that we don't like each other. Stems from when I worked for outlaws and gave the government a lot of trouble. I may have flipped sides, but that's not necessarily a victory for righteousness. This government tends to blur the lines between justice and crime. Too many political hands accepting cash from all directions, until the government's own policies become a tangled mess of inconsistencies.

Pops doesn't answer right away. He begins a "casual" stroll of the room. I know the old snake too well. The well-tailored suit, finer than most on the government's pay scale, implies to me that he's earned a high pay grade from the careers and lives he's ruined through his official duties. His dark eyes gaze everywhere in the room in a swift, efficient manner. Despite his gray hair, he's sharp as ever. Even his expanding midline would make someone underestimate how fast he can draw a gun or lunge…I know this from experience. His bulldog jowls give a better indication of his inner bite. By the time he pauses and stares at me, I wouldn't be surprised if he's guessed where my gun is hiding. He knows I con as much money winning marksmanship tournaments as I've won boxing matches.

"Brian DuWold," Pops speaks, "The URA has an assignment for you."

The initials are an interesting distinction. The United Republic is my birth country, and openly promotes its people and the values of freedom. But the extra "A" initial tacked on the end identifies the covert spy organization which performs the shady deeds needed to keep the country giving off a sunshine and rainbows appearance.

I ignore him for a few heartbeats as I reach for a couple heavy weights. Not the heaviest…I want to be able to throw them accurately if the conversation goes bad. "What noble purpose does the United Republic Agency wish me to serve?" I paused and turned a wary eye towards Pops. "At the usual payment fee of 'not enough'?"

Dongel interrupts, "There's always prison."

Dongel's personality is a contradiction to his partner. Pops can talk around a man until the opportunity to backstab is prime, Dongel is a bull who thinks he can just bash down any obstacle. The younger man stands straight and even rolls his shoulders in bravado. I don't doubt that he has muscles and reflexes, but I know he's going to bite off more than he can chew someday soon. Likely, with me. His usual demeanor is to threaten and intimidate. I have a feeling that one day we'll be going head-to-head when Pops isn't around to back him up.

Pops holds up a restraining hand to his partner, though he doesn't take his focus off me. "I did the favor of stopping by to check on your sister, Laurie. Poor girl, blind since birth if I recall? Most of her time is spent listening to the nurses read those books you send her, while she pets that pup. She's really fond of it; what did she name it?"

I dropped my gaze for a moment, readjusting the weights in my hands as a feint. I don't want them reading the expression on my face at that moment. Pops is treading a fine line between whether or not I'll be throwing one of these thirty-pound weights at his face. My parents surrendered my sister as a ward of the state as a baby, once her blindness was diagnosed. I've done my best to be a good big-brother, though government rules limit the help I can give.

I let the question hang too long in the air. Keeping my voice even, I respond. "Mugsly. She isn't allowed to keep pets, though."

Pops spoke in a friendly manner, but his face offered a stern look. "Nice how they found a way to bend the rules. At least…for now."

Pops apparently meant that as a reminder that all good situations can suddenly be reversed. I know the man's veiled threats all too well. I'd turn down thousands of dollars to do a job for them, but I'd reconsider if it meant helping out Laurie.

Pops continues, "That bend in the rules happened right after your Vicksburg escapade, wasn't it? Fortunate for us that a concerned citizen such as yourself took it upon himself to stop a notorious criminal, despite the collateral damage."

That was the cover story. Of course, the incident had been another assignment and Laurie's pup had been the reward. The fact that I don't have any official connection to the URA also absolved them of the five buildings that burned down in the process. But I did catch the arsonist and left them the body.

He reiterated, "Legally, we don't employ you. We don't even talk to you. At my latest account, you have 'Wanted' posters issued in at least three territories. I believe you've been charged with no less than eight crimes against the people."

"Some of that thanks to your own assignments."

"What assignments? We. Don't. Employ. You."

This argument will just go in circles, so I drop the weights on a bench and cut to the chase. "What assignment do you *not* have for me?"

Pops smiles, not the kind of smile that goes to his eyes. "We've come to talk to you about a war criminal. You are aware of Texico's application into the sovereignty of the United Republic?"

When Pops first started asking me to work for him, he assumed that I didn't know how to read, let alone be tuned in politics. He's come to know me as a guy who keeps an eye on all sorts of danger, even news stories and local rumors.

I know the United Republic already has influence stretching east-to-west, ocean-to-ocean. Texico is a region against the southern border. "Texico declared independence, revolted against Meztica and formed their own country, or so I've heard. Led by General Delbert Torres?"

Dongel clarifies, "*Governor* Torres, decorated hero of Texico, is pushing for it to become our newest territory. He has the support of his people."

I crack a smirk, "And we'll welcome them with open arms, as long as they also keep supplying that dark crud they leech from under their land."

Pops grabs the reins of the conversation, "Smart folks are calling it Black Gold, and for good reason. Oil is the resource of the future. Of course, it's just a bonus. The voluntary mixing of the people of Texico into the United Republic is reward enough for our future."

I can't help but smirk. It's amazing that Pops doesn't choke on the shit that exits his mouth. I turn to face him, "Of course. Now, where does this 'war criminal' come in?"

He continues, "Governor Torres' safety is paramount to the unification of our peoples. We're concerned for his well-being." Pops pulls a folded paper from a coat pocket. It unfolds, showing a portrait of a gray-haired man in a lab coat and protective gloves. "He has been threatened of late by a man who cast a dark shadow during the war: Dr. Gunter Nussbaum."

I almost snort at this particular turn of events. "I thought you had to fight for the opposing side to be considered a war criminal? Dr. Nussbaum partnered alongside General Torres, did he not? I've heard they unleashed horrors on the Meztican Army so terrible that most papers weren't printing details." At this I lean forward and look Pops squarely in the eye. "Or maybe the details were censored."

Dongel starts to make a move toward me, clenching his fists, but Pops puts out a hand. It wouldn't be the first time Dongel and I went nose to nose. Someday I'd love to test how well he can dance in a ring. It really rubs them that I can see through their bullshit and won't play nice with their games.

Once Dongel backs down, Pops returns his attention to me. The old snake adopts a tone suggestive of a teacher dealing with a recalcitrant pupil. "Governor Torres and Dr. Nussbaum both worked for independence, though not as cooperatively as some have suggested. The two men are quite disagreeable with each other." I sense a propaganda claim as Pops continues, "Since they won their freedom, the details of the doctor's repugnant experiments and techniques have come to light. People are outraged at his methods. The doctor is even reputed to have made the dead walk. He's reviled by those he recently liberated."

It doesn't surprise me that publicity and newspaper opinions tend to sway in a way favorable to the government. Not believing a word of any URA claims, I cross my arms and stare at a crack on the wall. Pops is doing a lot of moving and looking around the room as he talks. I think he's noticed my brass knuckles and still guessing at where my gun is hiding. He doesn't trust me, and I like it that way.

Pops continues. "Governor Torres banished him from Texico, along with his mutations. Unfortunately, the doctor didn't go far. We've had agents confirm he is plotting against the good people of Texico."

These government agents don't care so much for a pasture of sheep as much as the shepherd that leads the sheep. I decide to pin them on it, "You mean specifically, Torres?"

Pops nods, "Quite so. We caught wind of a planned assassination attempt. Also, we have reports of Nussbaum's intentions to turn Texico into his own atrocious, mutated paradise."

"Is the tipster someone I should know about?"

Pops throws a wink at Dongel, and flashes me a politician's smile, "So, you are interested in offering your services to the people?"

"'Interested' is a strong word." I glare at Pops, "We both know I'll be forced to go and that I'll regret it, so let's cut to the chase."

I notice Dongel has subtly shifted his stance to flank me, likely in case I balk or cause trouble. I actually have a trick up my sleeve in case he comes at that angle, but no sense in pushing a fight and forever being on the run.

Pops begins to reach for a cigar in his pocket, seems to think better of it, and lowers his hand. "The tipster is none other than Dr. Nussbaum's former pupil, Dr. Albert Ehrlichmann."

I roll my eyes. "That's a mouthful."

Pops just exposed the dark side of the government's plans. The former doctor isn't docile enough and too high profile. The younger doctor can offer them the same experiments and research without the burden of a bad reputation. Nussbaum was a heralded inventor prior to his feared war machines. I'm willing to take Pops' word at face value that there is trouble between Torres and Nussbaum. Like most of these 'assignments' I couldn't care if the URA suits get burned. On the other hand, most of the cases they bring to me tend to involve innocent people in harm's way. I'm a softie on that. I tend to like people despite themselves, even though once I get to know most folks I usually end up hating them. Well, except Jerry. That's because he helps me make a bunch of money just by taking my aggression out on other thugs.

I reach over and snatch a water glass that happens to sit next to my brass knuckles. The movement was casual enough, but it still startled Dongel into stepping forward. He stops as I sip the water.

I spare him a cool glance before addressing Pops. "Okay, so do I meet up with Dr…Albert?"

"Yes, he can advise you of the situation. You simply have to catch a train. Dr. Nussbaum's train, to be specific." Pops cracks a misleading smile.

So now I'm surprised again, "Why is he on Nussbaum's train? You just said he is helping you?"

"You weren't our first choice," Pops gives me a slow shake of the head. "We sent in a small team to find out more about Nussbaum's plans and stop him. Unfortunately, according to a rather boastful telegram we received from Dr. Nussbaum, only Ehrlichmann and one other member are still alive. He's using them as hostages. As far as the URA is concerned, it would be beneficial to receive Ehrlichmann alive, but both are expendable for the greater good of Texico's admission to the United Republic. Dr. Nussbaum proved during the war that he has no end to insidious devices, chemical bombs, and durable soldiers to carry out his plots. Whatever his specific attack plan is, we no longer care; we know it involves this train and that's good enough. Getting you to his train and stopping him is our primary concern."

The admission of a failed team and the revelation of me as an unplanned back-up dips this whole situation into a flaming outhouse. They're desperate and I'm the one who has to pull out a last-minute save or take the fall for it.

I mutter, "Who else from your expert team survived?"

The old snake spreads his arms wide. "We don't know. Nussbaum's train left San Golbriel yesterday morning, headed for Texico's capital. There isn't much time to waste before he reaches Austren. You're one of the few assets in the area left to us."

I envision the lay of the land in my head, even as my mind bristles at being an 'asset.' What he's suggesting can't be done. "Even if I had a relay chain of fresh horses, I couldn't get ahead of the train or hope to catch it before it reaches Austren."

Pops grins, "We know you're an educated man who hears gossip and reads between the lines. Haven't you heard rumors about our experiments to prepare lighter-than-air vehicles for combat?"

Now I'm worried, and I can't hide it from showing. "Airplanes? I've heard of some, but they're a novelty. Flimsy wood and canvas frames? One person can fly them a few hundred feet? Can't say as I've ever seen one that could outrace a horse."

Dongel continues to glare as Pops reaches over and throws my shirt at me. "You're about to see one that can do just that."

*　　*　　*

Events speed up after that. I finish cleaning up, don a nice suit, pocket the brass knuckles and buckle on my six-shooter. I advise Jerry to get a cut of the action in the casinos at Palmera, where I hope to catch up with him later. It should be a safe location if another war breaks out at the capital. Of course, he's not happy with the situation, but there's no choice here. The URA suits escort me outside. We walk on the boardwalk to avoid the horses and wagons churning up the muddy street. A guy at a corner with posters is hawking interest in the newest invention: a horseless carriage he calls an automobile. A bunch of cowboys throw out insults, enjoying a few laughs over this guy's fantasy.

I can't help but look at it and think the world is changing. The nineteenth century is heading to a conclusion. The factories and machine inventions that sprang to life during the United Republic's Civil War has propelled society into new directions. It seems that coming up with new technology to quell rebellions has a way of bolstering progress. Steam inventions, electricity, magnetism…new marvels are being introduced into our lifestyle every year and I'm beginning to feel outdated.

At the other end of town, we walk past a line of lawmen guarding a lone, large barn. No one else is allowed past the line, or even near it. I bet most of those lawmen don't even have a clue what may be inside. I'm not sure I want to know what's in there. Pops pulls out a set of keys and opens the lock. In no time we're inside and they're relocking the outer door.

The inside of the barn has been gutted in order to fit the new centerpiece. I've seen newspaper printings of skeletal wood-and-paper flying machines, but this is something very different. A long, cylindrical tub makes up the central body. There's a combination of wood planks and thin metal plates forming it. I assume the large holes in the top are seats, accommodating more than one rider. It rests on wheels that look like they've been taken from a bicycle. A double set of wings stretch out from the front, one set under and one set over the central tub. Three smaller wings branch off the tail end: one rising up, two others spread to the sides. A big fan with four blades is mounted in front of the tub. Gears and belts are visible through a propped-open lid near the fan. Work tools sit on a nearby bench. Studying a contraption mounted on top of the front, I realize it looks like a pair of those Gatling guns that won Texico's independence. I've seen one such gun before, with a tall, rectangular magazine on top which held the bullets. Sure enough, there is a revolving device standing upright over each gun, holding a few such magazines. Once the driver finishes shooting through one, they must somehow rotate the device so that the next magazine swings into place.

I can see a few drawbacks on the design. For one, it probably obstructs some of the driver's forward view. Helps to see what you're shooting. Second, the twin guns are aiming through the front fan blades. Hopefully they have something fixed up to coordinate the two, or the guns would shred the capability of flight. A similar, solitary Gatling gun is mounted rear-facing from the last hole in the tub. The airplane is painted mostly blue and white, but it has a name written across the side: *Liberty Flyer*.

I turn to Dongel and smile in a manner to irritate him, "Nice toy, too bad that bulky thing won't get off the ground. You expect me to roll to the capital?"

"Who said that!?" Exclaims a voice from the other side of the craft.

A head pops up and looks over the body of the airplane. A *female* head, with long, dark hair, but otherwise not looking too pretty. I can see one of her hands resting on top of the tub, holding a wrench.

The grimace must be plain on my face. "You got an old mare working on this thing?"

She scowls and yells back, "Don't tell me you have problems with folks who don't have their brain dangling between their legs!"

The woman starts tromping around the airplane and toward me. I can see she wears a leather jacket and canvas pants. Tall riding boots adorn her feet. She looks rather plain, not the type who would normally turn my head in a crowd. Of course, the angry glare in her eyes doesn't help her looks. Pops interposes between us. She stops with hands on her hips, holding onto that glare. Her spark is the one thing I can respect. She's brave enough to look me in the eyes as if she wants to go a few rounds in the ring with me, despite my towering height and bulk.

Pops makes introductions. "Jane, this is Brian DuWold."

"Boxer," I interrupt.

"He'll be your passenger. Mr. DuWold, this is Jane Emerson. She owns a fair share of Texico's abundant oil fields. Mrs. Emerson funded this aircraft research." He pauses before driving his last point home. "She is also the one who operates it."

"This dame drives that contraption? That thing doesn't look like it could get off the ground, and the guns are positioned to shoot off the fan blades."

Pops starts to reply, "Contraption? You should see it in action. As I told you, oil is the future…"

"I'm the *pilot*," Dame talks right over him. "It runs on an internal combustion engine. It flies. When I want to shoot, the engine replaces the old crank lever that normally fires those guns. That allows it to time the shots between propeller blades. And if you aren't impressed, *Boxer*," she makes the nickname sound derogatory, "why don't I take off and we'll duel. You stand on the ground with that compensatingly big revolver and shoot up at me with your six bullets. I'll fly out of your range and spray you with *sixty* rounds in twenty seconds."

During her short litany, she unknowingly distracts me when she starts rolling up a cigarette. I can smell the plane's fuel on her gloves as she lights it. Keeping my outward calm, I ask, "And will that be good enough to stop Dr. Nussbaum's train?"

"These will." She raises her boot and taps an oval-like object hanging under the bottom wings.

I hadn't noticed it before. I lean over and glance under the body to note an identical object mounted opposite. "Bombs?" I look at them doubtfully. Are they packed with TNT? "They look small. What's in them?"

Pops answers, "We don't know. Those two bombs are Dr. Ehrlichmann's addition to the project. It's some liquid-based explosive. Upon impact, the liquids mix and create a crater that could swallow small buildings. It should stop any train. Care must be taken to avoid rough handling, or," he looks pointedly at Dame and her cigarette, "flames."

She blows a smoke ring in his face as she taps off a few ashes from the cigarette. They sprinkle sparks over the metal-cased bomb. Pops and Dongel reflexively step back. I think Dame is crazy, but it's hard to dislike someone too much when they scare those suits as well as I can. Maybe better.

I can think of a lot of holes in their plan and I'm likely being kept out of all the details, but I'm not one who wastes time tackling a problem from every angle. "Well, the sooner we crash and explode, the sooner this job is done. Let's get to it."

*   *   *

We fly through the night. It isn't easy to speak over the rushing wind, and neither Dame nor I feel particularly talkative, so much of the journey passes in silence. It's not like we sit too close together anyway. Dame is up front in the driver's seat. Behind her is a single, long, open hatch converted from a cargo space into room for two more possible passengers. Behind it all, I'm sitting at the tail gun, facing the wrong way. It's too dark to see the ground. Most of this region is open, dry land anyway. It's likely just rocks, scrub brush, rattlesnakes and jackrabbits. I get tired of seeing only smoke and stars pass by; the only thing changing is the hypnotic sway of the tail rudder. Once I realize we aren't going to crash, I catch a little sleep. A tinge of lighter sky could be visible in the east as Dame yells for my attention. She's pointing to a patch of white below us. It resembles the smoke trail billowing out of a train funnel as it travels.

"Dame! This Gatling back here, is it controlled by the engine as well?"

I can barely hear her over the wind. "It doesn't need to be timed because it swivels, and the propellers aren't back there. See the hand crank on the side? That's your trigger. Don't shoot the rudder off!"

Of course, the rudder is standing in the middle of my view. I yell, "This thing can shoot the rudder off?" To which she basically repeats her last sentence, though doubled in length due to the addition of several unladylike words.

We drop down to identify the train. It's hard to see details, but we come to the conclusion that the engine has a very odd, ominously big outline. The cars are all uniformly painted dark gray, with no identifying markings. The silhouette of a large gun sticks out from the caboose. We watch as a lit door opens between coaches, and an armed figure wearing some weird, leather mask steps from one car to the next. Hopefully no one down there sees us flying in the night sky.

"That's them!" She calls. Her hands maneuver the stick, aligning the plane on a course that should sneak up from the rear. "I'm going to drop the bombs on the engine!"

I look over my shoulder, watching her progress, when a thought hits me. I've noticed a lot of handholds running the length of the fuselage, and even into the wings.

"Dame, what's the deal with all these handles and bars running along everything?"

She turns her face, a puzzled look meeting my eyes. "I've had this idea that folks will pay big money to see someone walk on the wings of an airplane in flight. I've tried it and had those rails installed for just that purpose."

A plan has been forming in my head, and those rails give me the ability to carry it out. "Don't bomb them yet! Fly low over the train so I can drop down."

"Are you crazy?"

I probably am. But I never take what those suits say at face value. They've cost me a lot of freedom with half-truths over the years. I'm eager to take a peek at the doctor and his hostages. I'd like to know more about what's going on. I sum this up nicely for my confused pilot. "Yes!"

Liberty Flyer has been steadily overtaking the slower moving locomotive. The train isn't very long, but it still has about sixteen cars attached. Dame is already flying over the rear ones, which look like tankers. I start climbing out of my seat, trying to convince myself this isn't the craziest thing I've ever done. Actually, it isn't. Sadly, I've got no time to reminisce about the weekend in Les Orellas involving the steamboat casino, the midget, the one-legged rodeo girl, and the horse with that bean-gas problem.

I need all my concentration here. I've never felt wind blast me so hard. A few rails on the side of the plane's tub offer handholds. No looking down. My eyes stay fixed on the parts of the plane I can grab as I make my way down.

I hang off the bottom of the airplane, offering me a nice view of the two bombs. The train cars rumble right below, though Dame's trying to line up directly over them. The track has a few curves to it, and sometimes the airplane's momentum has me swinging side to side. Train smoke blows into my face. It seems like it's a short enough fall, but everything's moving out of tandem as I watch car after car pass by. The tankers are left behind and now I'm dangling over boxcars. My arms are straining as I try to time a good jump. No, not yet. Not that one. Maybe, no, I don't like the angle. Shoot, I'm going to run out of cars soon.

Ahead, a hatch pops open atop one of the cars. A figure emerges, looking around. He wears one of those weird leather masks on his head. He's looking the wrong way, but the airplane is coming up on him fast. He'll either see or hear us any moment. I drop my right hand free, reach into my pocket and slip on one of my personalized brass knuckles. He's turning in my direction. I don't like the angle of the jump…

…but then I fall anyway.

His masked face softens the landing of my fist; his body crumples under my weight. I scramble to hold something as I slide towards the side edge. My leg hooks the hatch and my hands grab hold of the man, who's trapped half in and out of the hatch. I pull myself to a sitting position on the edge of the entry. The man is still breathing, though it sounds odd because it's too loud. He's not moving. I use one hand to rip the mask away, but it's still dark out. Something occurs to me: the breathing sound is coming from the mask and an apparatus on his chest, not from him. There hasn't been any alarm or response from inside the train car, so I take a moment to investigate. I always carry a lighter just in case there is a need, so I whip it out now and light it to take a look. I hold it in close to him as the flame flickers in the wind.

The bluish-gray face I look upon seems to have lost the humanity it once possessed. In place of eyes, he has some kind of mirrored lenses grafted to his skin. I can see my reflection but nothing past the lens…probably a good thing. It's like looking at a corpse, but this corpse is breathing. His breaths are shallow and ragged. I glance at the mask. With each 'breath' of the mask, a puff of noxious fume comes out. I have a feeling it wouldn't be good for me to breathe it in. I glance down at the guy's hands. At first it looked like he's wearing a clawed glove, then I realize they are fingerless gloves. He has metal claws somehow grafted to the end of his fingers.

The suits' words come back to me. Dr. Nussbaum was reputed to have made the dead walk. I can understand where that story originated. This guy doesn't exactly seem dead, but his life clearly is no longer his to command.

I look for Dame's airplane. She's abandoned her bombing run, currently flying off to the side. There's no telling how long she'll wait before doing something, so I need to move. I dump the body over the side of the train. I put my ear down into the hatch enough to listen in; I can hear another figure moving down there. I'm on top of the coaches and they all have roof hatches, so I decide to make use of them. The cars may be full of soldiers, but if I stay up top and glance through the hatches, hopefully I can avoid trouble. I traverse a walkway on top of the train and move forward. The train shifts constantly as I grope ahead in the dark.

It takes precious long time to get to the next hatch and lay flat against it. My hands work slowly, loosening the top. Lucky for me, it's unlatched. I slowly ease the lid and peer inside. For a train car, the interior is dressed to the décor of a mansion. Wood panels with a buffalo-print motif on the sides; a plush rug covering the floor. This half of the coach seems to be an office. A wall and a door block my view of anything further up the coach. A gaunt figure in a lab coat grabs my attention straight ahead. I believe I'm looking at Dr. Nussbaum.

A thin layer of gray hairs dominates his head. He wears glasses, has ink stains his fingers, and those sparse hairs curl every direction. I think he gave up on combs. His long coat carries all manner of papers and writing utensils, with small journals sticking out of the pockets. His face exhibits more wrinkles than a pug dog I once owned, but not near as cute. All in all, a guy who didn't have enough luck chasing women or enjoying the outside as a kid. I'm guessing his hands never worked as hard as mine have. He's sitting behind a desk even more cluttered than his pockets, though I can see most of him well-enough from my angle. A gun rests in his lap. He's talking to someone right below me, though I can't look down well enough to see them. Whoever they are, they wouldn't be able to see his gun from their angle. I count four empty coffee mugs on his desk, reminding me of the early hour. I suppose when the government tries to kill you, and you're en route to commence your master plan, sleep just gets in the way.

"So what was their bribe, Ehrlichmann? Gold?"

"*Doctor* Ehrlichmann!" Stresses a voice below me, out of sight.

"Pah! You are a student! Everything you've made was stolen from my inventiveness!" Nussbaum and Ehrlichmann are speaking the same accent, though I can't pinpoint their origins. Nussbaum continues his rant. "You sided with the usurper! *I* won independence! *I* scared Meztica away! Texico owes me its loyalty and obedience!"

The hidden voice beneath me screeches back, "You couldn't succeed without my help! If it wasn't for me, you'd still be postulating chemical theorems! You never gave me due credit. You seek only a slave state, rather than the greater partnership and resources available from the United Republic! I set my goals higher than you, because you could never appreciate the overall possibilities!"

Dr. Ehrlichmann's voice runs thick with ambition. I can't help but wonder about my earlier concerns. The suits won't have the senior doctor because of his bad reputation, but the junior one might be more susceptible to suggestions. As I sort my thoughts, Nussbaum suggests something along those very same lines.

Ehrlichmann becomes outraged. His voice practically shrieks. "And what is your goal once you have your slave state? You think you can sit in your corner of the world undisturbed? The URA won't control me, but it pays to let someone with resources think they are in charge!" Ehrlichmann yells as he admits his desires. "They know I can make the United Republic the most powerful country on the planet. Even their precious oil will pale compared to our, I mean *my*, research. The URA can be the perfect tool to be exploited."

Nussbaum stands and holds the gun at his side. There is no way Dr. Ehrlichmann could miss seeing it now. "Your self-adulations are a bit premature. I hold you at my whim. The URA won't respond in time to stop me from wiping Torres from memory. I find myself less and less agreeable to staying your executions. Let them think I still hold you alive, that hesitation will cost them. They can't stop me!"

A new speaker comes into the conversation from below, hidden from my sight. It surprises me to hear a pleasant female voice. "Good doctor, you still think of me as an enemy? How that hurts me so!"

I notice Nussbaum's expression soften. He glances to someone who seems to be standing by Dr. Ehrlichmann, and addresses her. "Perhaps you were misled; maybe the URA did use you just to get on board. It would certainly be their modus operandi. However, I can't afford to trust you, dear." Nussbaum turns back to the table. He fishes out a small gun from beneath a sheaf of papers. He holds a tiny pocket pistol in his free hand. It has two barrels, and likely holds one bullet per barrel. I'm familiar with the type of gun; however, this version has attachments and gadgetry I've never seen. Nussbaum continues, "You tried to conceal this from my soldiers! The gun you possessed has Ehrlichmann's signature handiwork in the inventions adorning it. These adaptations are from my own designs."

She speaks again, an edge of tears in her voice. "I'm no threat. Allow me time to get you in touch with my editor. You'll see I was unknowingly sent in with the agency."

As I watch the emotions battle across Nussbaum's face, it's clear he wants to believe her despite the rather obvious evidence to the contrary. She must be very persuasive.

She implores the doctor. "I know once I write a story on you, the truth will come out. The people will understand your position and mistreatment by the government. Many don't trust the URA as it is! Let them see your side of the story. Educate the uninformed masses! I can turn public opinion behind you. Please don't shoot me."

By that point she almost has me convinced the URA is the enemy and Nussbaum is some shining white knight. But then I recall the zombie-like soldier. Even without that image, my gut tells me the woman is just playing with Nussbaum's buttons.

It seems she's succeeding because Nussbaum seems shame-faced about the threats he made. Instead of confronting her head-on, he turns his attention back to Ehrlichmann. "Well, I can't afford to let you live, my student. But, maybe you can help Miss Ferns' story."

Something about that name rings familiar in my head, but I can't place it. Nussbaum continues. "If you write a confession, one I can use to combat the plots and lies against me, I will offer you a swift death. You won't have to feel the taste of immortality behind a gas mask. As much as your betrayal wounds me, I can be merciful."

Ehrlichmann refuses to back down. He responds in a demanding tone in another language. As he practically spits out his message, Nussbaum turns a deep shade of red.

"Ooh! Ooh! Good doctor?" The woman speaks excitedly, and Nussbaum's attention is drawn back to her. "We should get a photograph of you capturing this URA spy! That will help your public image."

Dr. Nussbaum clearly has some reservations on his mind. He indulges in private contemplation for a moment before sheepishly nodding to the unseen woman. "A photograph never hurts. Publicity or not, I would enjoy keeping a visual record in my archives of the moment my traitorous student stared down the barrel of my gun. Fetch her camera!"

One of those masked, armed soldiers lumbers into view from where he must have been standing near the prisoners. He stops at the table, looks blankly at it for a moment before leaning stiffly over to pick up a small box. I'm used to cameras being big, bulky accordion-like devices carried on tripods, but this device could be easily held in the hands.

As all this unfolds below me, my thoughts move toward putting a bullet through Nussbaum's forehead. However, what about my ability to rescue either hostage? I don't think saving Ehrlik…Erlich…Al's life might be worth risking my hide. He strikes me as being too similar to his mentor for the greater good. But what about the woman? Is she telling any truth? How is she mixed up in this? Nussbaum steps around his desk, standing below the hatch. I watch as he strikes a pose for the lady, firmly staring down the gun at his former partner in crime.

FLASH!

I'm seeing stars! Ghostly lights swim across my vision yet I wasn't even looking at the camera. Both doctors blather animatedly in their native language. My eyes clear enough to see Nussbaum has dropped both his gun and Miss Ferns'. He stumbles back into his desk. The guard is staggering near one side-wall, arms reaching blindly. A slender hand reaches from the unseen area below me as Miss Ferns reclaims her dropped pocket shooter from the floor. I realize I'm already about two seconds late; I should have drawn my gun and shot my target.

I reach for my gun, glancing at my holster. In that moment, I hear the BOOM of a small cannon or such coming from below. With my revolver ready in my right hand, I throw the top hatch all the way open to give me easier access. I've obviously missed something important. Nussbaum is still staggering around his desk. I can't see Al. On the other hand, I do see a pair of strikingly nice legs ending in petite women's shoes lying on the floor. Most shocking of all, the guard and most of the wall behind him are missing. I force myself to concentrate on the doctor. As my sights line up, he slams his hand on a button on his desk.

Several clear, glass panes swing into place between his desk and this side of the coach room. A pull of the trigger and my gun kicks into my hand. It's one of the most powerful handguns made, the recoil can break a dainty wrist, but the bullet barely chips the first layer glass Nussbaum is now hiding behind. As I stare in disbelief, I see a vial thrown at the window, presumably an attack from Doctor Al. A smoking liquid splashes across the surface. It does little harm to the glass but begins to melt holes in the wooden floor.

"A gunshot?!" Miss Ferns exclaims.

"Curse you, Nut Tree!" Ehrlichmann rants, focused on his adversary. "This hasn't ended!"

"Of course not!" Nussbaum declares as he exits the far door, safe behind his barrier. He's rubbing his eyes and staggering off balance. "It ends in five minutes when my guards swarm you."

I'm gripping both my gun and the rocking hatch as I figure out what to do. We're still on a moving train. I hear and see Dame fly by overhead. She probably heard my shot. Even if she didn't, she's on the side where she can see the hole blasted in the side of the coach. I return my attention to the scene below. "Is everyone alright down there?"

Miss Ferns steps into view. The pocket gun is in one hand and the camera tucked under an arm. She is knockout pretty. Her tailored outfit looks fashionable, her blouse reveals an enticing bit of cleavage, a belt ties her dress around an hourglass waist. Her dress has fallen back down enough to hide those perfect legs. Ferns' eyes are like two blue diamonds, demurely peeking out of the shade of her feathered hat. Her lightly blushed cheeks meet at a pair of full lips colored in forbidden-fruit red. I finally realize I've been staring.

The moment is broken as a spindly, gray-haired man shuffles into view, muttering, "What buffoon did they send to help me now?" He looks up at me through a pair of thick spectacles. He's wearing a light-tan trench coat and business-like pants. Pencils stick out of his coat pocket. "I say, you couldn't have gotten here a little sooner?"

My glare should express my emotions, though I also add, "I just jumped from an airplane to get here. You must be Al."

That sets him off so much that he hisses air through his gritted teeth to reply. "Doctor Albert Ehrlich…"

"I know. You're Al." My eyes swivel to meet the beautiful one. "I never caught your first name."

"Sally. Miss Sally Ferns, *People's Daily*."

She throws me the most wondrous smile and even manages a curtsey. Now I know why her name rang a bell. She's a popular reporter for one of the biggest newspapers and she's written a few books. Of course, at this point it's only proper that I respond, but I rarely give out my real name. Normally I'd tip my hat, but one hand has a gun and the other is holding the hatch open. "Brian DuWold. Most call me Boxer." How did my real name slip out?

Ehrlichmann sneers, "Well, *Boxer*. Get me off this train now, if you can, then go kill Dr. Nussbaum."

It seems everyone wants to make my nickname sound derogatory. I have to delay any response, because one of Nussbaum's 'gasmask' soldiers is on the rooftop walkway coming from the front of the train. He fires a rifle, though his shot pings against the raised steel hatch. I aim, fire, and watch as he rocks back a step. He starts walking toward me again, firing another round past my head. I can't think of a single guy who could stay standing once I've punched one through their chest like that. The last guy's head was vulnerable when I landed, so I line my sights up with the forehead. This time his head snaps back and he falls like a rag doll off the roof.

I vault over the hatch and spin around. A bullet strikes it from the rear, as two more of those zombies walk toward me from behind. I give them two more shots from my revolver. Both of them topple, staring into the new skylights I put into their gasmasks.

That leaves only an airplane flying at me from the rear. I let the hatch close as I drop prone. I hear the ratatatatat of *Liberty Flyer*'s double guns as Dame skims a few feet over the roof of the train. Hot casings rain past me. The barrage lasts about twenty seconds and I know without looking the train has sixty holes strafed along its length. Probably got Nussbaum upset by now, hopefully dead. If nothing else, my car passes a couple limp soldiers rolling to a stop alongside the tracks.

The eastern sky is brightening up. Even if Dame didn't just rake the train with bullets, it would be easy for anyone on board to spot her now. I'm not sure how many Dame knocked off with her attack. The roof of the train seems momentarily clear of anyone but me. It's time to get Miss Ferns and Al off the train so Dame can drop a couple bombs on it.

I throw open the hatch, "Coming down!" And promptly drop in between them.

As soon as I land, the back door of the coach opens up. I make sure my brass knuckle is settled in one fist while my gun swings around at the threat. It's another masked soldier. In the light of the coach at this range I can see his mirrored eyes behind the mask goggles. Before he can raise his rifle far enough, I touch my barrel to his head and ventilate his mask. He stumbles into a second soldier standing in the doorway. My gun fixes on him.

Click.

Back-up plan. I give him a left hook with the knuckle that drops him between coaches. He falls into a place where I don't need to worry about him anymore.

"What do we do now, sir?" That sweet voice asks.

I let loose the spent casings from my revolver and load the cylinders with rounds stored on my gun belt. "We need to get off this train before that airplane drops a couple bombs on it."

The doctor's demeanor dramatically changes. A mad smile dominates his face. "Success! Emerson was actually able to get it in the air with those bombs on board? My calculations couldn't guarantee it would happen."

I stare at him real hard, slapping the reloaded cylinder back into place.

He notices my hard glare and collects his thoughts. "A needed gamble, Boxer. Plenty of lives are at stake. One must risk the occasional setback for the needs of progress."

As I look at the doctor, I notice a rope running the length of the coach above his head. I lay a hand on it.

Noticing my intent, Al argues, "This is Dr. Nussbaum's train. He's packed it with soldiers, weapons, toxic chemicals and nasty surprises. It's on track to deliver a huge bomb at the capital. It isn't going to stop if you pull the emergency cord!"

I pull the cord. Seconds later, we hear the screech of brakes and the billow of steam as the train slows down. I'm sure it's not often that the mad doctor looks so perplexed.

I shrug, "Maybe he forgot to relay that important information to whatever zombies he has operating the train."

The doctor shakes his head, mumbling, "Nut Tree."

Out of the corners of my eyes I'm watching the terrain slow down through the huge hole in the wall. My last match put me at 6'4", with a wingspan almost one foot wider. I could easily stretch my arms across this hole from side to side, and from shoulders to shins. I wish I hadn't missed whatever created that explosion when I glanced away earlier.

The doctor's words catch up to my thoughts. I ask him, "You said 'nut tree' before. What are you talking about?"

"That's what his name means in the olde language. Nussbaum…Nut Tree." Suddenly he laughs like it's the funniest joke he's heard all day. "It fits him perfectly! Crazy as a tree full of nuts! For example, he insisted on that inefficient gas mask technique of induction, rather than my proven method of a permanent endotracheal insertion."

I must have a blank look on my face. Miss Ferns is politely nodding, but I have the feeling she's as perplexed as me. When the doctor realizes it, he motions at the dead guard's mask with its noxious gas streaming out of the bullet hole. "For his minions. He was worried about the public reaction to the augmented faces of these walking cadavers, so he chose to just cover them with those smelly masks instead. Inefficient! Waste of material and time!"

Feeling pretty disgusted, I ask, "So, are they actually living men, or really the walking dead?"

This seems to amuse the doctor. He manages to speak between chuckling, "Essentially, they are alive, but it isn't life as you'd know it. They don't feel pain, thus can continue performing their duties when a normal person would falter. All come from prisons, or are war criminals, or sometimes just former critics of Dr. Nussbaum. All put to good use!"

I decide I really don't like this man any more than Nussbaum. I switch the subject. "And your name means?"

He stands up proud as a peacock at that moment. "Honest man."

"Al means honest man?"

Miss Ferns doesn't stifle a giggle. The doctor goes red in the face. "Ehrlichmann means Honest Man! *Doctor* Ehrlichmann."

"Ok, Al." I wave at the hole in the wall. "We've made it to our stop."

The doctor walks over to the blasted hole and steadies himself against part of the wreckage, staring out. "The train hasn't stopped yet!"

His reply tells me what my sense of balance already knows. "It's speeding up again. Now is the time." The doctor sputters a protest. I see something outside and comment. "A creek! Nice, soft landing. Here you go!"

I kick him out. By that time, the creek has already passed and he lands in a spray of gravel. I turn to Miss Ferns as I tuck my gun away and slip my brass knuckles back into my pocket. She steps forward bravely, her fine dress rippling in the wind. Her eyes are filled with fright as she says. "This is going to hurt."

Her words seem to melt through my hard shell. "Hopefully me more than you." I scoop her into a tight hug and throw one more glance where we're headed. I fall backward; she's frail and tucked firmly in my embrace as my back skims the gravel like a skipping stone. Yeah, it hurts.

We skid to a stop and I finally let go. She scampers off of me. I can see she's worried for my health even before she speaks. "Are you okay, Mr. Boxer? Here, stand up if you can and let me take a look."

'Mr. Boxer?' I don't think anyone has ever addressed me in that manner. I like it. As soon as I stand, Miss Ferns walks behind me and she sucks in her breath with a hiss. The morning light isn't that great, but I imagine its good enough to illuminate whatever is causing that fiery pain along my back. Feels like the worst case of sunburn I've ever had. I catch sight of Al limping toward us, trench coat torn, pencils missing, his hair scattered like an upended bird's nest. The sound of *Liberty Flyer* passing overhead reminds me of the urgent situation. I also hear the squealing and hissing sounds of the train's brakes, which means more problems in our near future.

"He knows we've jumped off!" After I shout, I glance around and spot a dilapidated train station, as well as a couple barns and corrals near it. I assume that during parts of the year a rancher could pen his cattle here to load onto a train. Just past the buildings and corrals is a packed dirt trail. It would make a good landing strip for Dame. "This way. Run!"

We get halfway to the first corral. I run while keeping eyes on Al and Miss Fern, both running as best they can, but still minutes from the road. The train has come to a full stop. One of the box cars is opening slowly. Not just a sliding door, either. The opposing walls are lowering, revealing something stacked in framework.

Dr. Ehrlichmann looked back and saw it as well. "Run! He's unloading the steamcycles!"

Steamcycles? Still watching the train, I notice Dame's plane strafing it again. This time, several turrets have popped up along parts of the roof. Machine guns aboard the train return fire. *Liberty Flyer* banks away before finishing her run. I'm wishing she would have dropped the bombs but it looks like she's turning around to line up with the trail to land and pick us up.

Miss Ferns and Al are ahead of me, sprinting through the corral fences. I reach the first one when I hear a noise behind me. Turning back, I see something out of a madman's imagination.

They call a train the iron horse, but this new contraption speeding at me seems more apt for the name. The main body runs on two wheels, front and back, blowing off an angry hiss of smoke behind it. A driver straddles it like a horse, but he's leaning into a pair of handles up front. A bin, looking like a partly covered wheelbarrow, attaches to one side and has a third, smaller wheel on its side for balance. A soldier sits in the side bin, holding a rifle and pointing it my direction. There are several more following the leader. I can tell they'll run us down before we can get aboard the airplane.

The airplane! Dame's already landing, and those bombs are going to be very vulnerable on the ground.

I run around the corner of a barn. Miss Fern and Al are kicking up dust as they lead the way to the road, but they can't outrun our pursuer. Inside the bar is a stall. I shrug off the discomfort in my back as I lift my leg and kick one end of a wooden plank loose. I hastily wrench the plank free, throw it over my shoulder and stumble under its weight back to the barn door. I pick an ambush position just inside the barn door.

Through an open shutter, I spot Miss Fern stumble. Al doesn't help her up; he steps over her and keeps running. From the other direction, I can hear the mechanical rhythm of the steamcycle roaring closer. The steam whistles out like a coffee kettle signaling a boil and is bearing down faster than a race horse.

I risk a peek out the door just in time to act. The masked driver of the steamcycle is focused on the fallen woman and doesn't see me swinging a two-by-four into his face. The wood splinters and pulls out of my hands. It sprays in pieces beyond me, landing alongside the cart-wheeling, rag-doll flailing driver. The side-bin soldier looks over his shoulder at me as the speeding cycle continues forward. The main body of the bike proves lucky as it passes alongside the open tailgate of someone's abandoned buckboard wagon, but the side-bin soldier isn't so lucky. The folks on the train probably hear the noise as his head smacks the wagon's tailgate. I run to catch up with the slowing steamcycle, stooping to pick up the rifle next to the body twitching under the wagon's tailgate. The other steamcycles are well behind, but they'll catch us soon enough.

I throw the rifle into the side bin in case it comes in handy later. I jump aboard the rolling bike and start working the handle controls. After a few unpleasant noises of grinding gears and hissing exhaust, I finally figure how to go forward and how to stop. Not quite in that order. In moments I'm catching up to the beautiful lady and the madman scientist running next to her. I glance around looking for Dame. *Liberty Flyer* is on the trail, trying to turn around to make use of the straightest path. In order to take off, she'll have to roll back toward the gang of steamcycles—a gang of steamcycles likely driven by zombie-like soldiers oblivious to a fear of death.

One problem at a time.

I pull up alongside Miss Ferns and Al. "Hop on!"

Of course, I situated myself near the lovely reporter first. Hiking up her dress just a little, she walks up behind me. Ignoring the side-bin, she puts one delicate hand on my shoulder and hops up on the seat behind me, side-saddle. In order to hang on, she wraps her arms around my waist and presses herself against my back. This sets my back on fire again, but I can tolerate it. I can feel her softness snuggling against me, which manages to block any discomfort.

Then the doctor runs up and gives her a shove. She topples, landing rump-first in the side-seat with her legs stuck in the air, oriented to face backward. The spindly armed doctor jumps on and climbs halfway up my back, reaching around and clutching me in a death grip. At least one pocket pencil survived, jabbing into my raw back. "Get me out of here! I need to live and have my revenge on Nut Tree!"

Gritting my teeth in pain, I accelerate as fast as I can. I send a rooster tail of mud and rocks spinning in the air toward our pursuers as I make for the airplane. A rush of air, faster than any horse ride, whips past. "How many are back there?" I hiss through my teeth.

Miss Ferns, stuck in an awkward position, is able to see what's behind us. "Four cycles. All of them riding double."

The doctor shouts some curse in his native language, followed by "He means to recapture me!"

In seconds I'm bringing the cycle to a sudden, shuddering stop alongside the parked plane. The abruptness doesn't affect Miss Ferns because she's tucked into the side-bin enough that it doesn't bother her. The doctor, however, flips over my back and slides in the dust. I swear it was an accident. I am completely mollified.

The steamcycles are closing in fast. I hear Dame cursing, "Why did you lead his soldiers here?"

I yell back, "Why didn't you bomb the train before landing?"

With no answer coming, I extract Miss Ferns from the contraption and turn her toward the waiting airplane. Al is already scrambling into the converted cargo opening behind Dame, yelling for her "to just go." I turn around, drawing my revolver.

Unfortunately, the cycles are already right there and slowing to a stop. They are sitting squarely in the takeoff path of the plane. The four zombie soldiers in the side bins climb out with their rifles pointed at me. The four drivers disembark with a stiff-jointed rhythm and draw pistols. Leather creaks as they step out in a line, or maybe it's their deathlike joints creaking. Eight soldiers coming at me, but only six bullets in my gun. I slide my left fist into my pocket, fingers fitting into place inside the brass knuckles. Unfortunately, the guards are still far enough away to make fists seem pointless. I recall the ones I faced down earlier: anything short of a headshot may not drop these guys.

Miss Ferns' voice startles me. The reporter never took her cue to head for the plane, and she's still standing a couple feet away. Oddly enough, she holds up that small box camera of hers. "Dr. Nussbaum's infamous zombie soldiers and their steamcycles! I have to get a photograph of this!"

FLASH!

Once again, I'm not even looking at the flash and I'm seeing ghostly stars swimming in front of my vision. The riders seem to fare worse. They've stopped still as statues. The only movements they seem capable of are head twitches. That has to be one uniquely-modified camera.

Guessing that's my cue. I start pulling the trigger, fanning the hammer back with my knuckle hand. One drops. Through the smoke of the first shot, I pop another round through the head of the second one. I run down the line, shooting fast. The soldiers are barely moving. Two of them reach forward like they're blindly trying to feel ahead. I hear shots going off behind me. One soldier drops dead even as I'm swinging my sights toward him. Skipping on to the next in line, I drop him with a hot round. The one beyond him also drops to the mystery gunner. The last soldier takes a slight stumble forward, making me miss. My gun clicks, all rounds gone, but the other shooter drops him. All eight are embracing the dirt. I turn and look over my shoulder. Dame casually holds up a revolver, sitting in the cockpit of the airplane. She gives me a cool glare as she blows the smoke coming from the muzzle.

I pocket my weapons before I reach a hand down to help Miss Ferns up. In all the gunfire she had dropped to her knees and covered her ears. Once she's up, I stoop over and retrieve her camera. I want to say something better than, "Nice camera," but that's all that comes out.

She blushes, "Thank you kindly. My departed pa, an inventor, made it."

I run over and start moving steamcycles. Al shows he has the smarts to realize these things need to go in order to clear the trail. We start each one and send it rolling off the side. A quick glance toward the train yields no more surprises inbound, but I'm not trusting my luck today.

I gracefully catch up to the airplane as Al scrambles onboard, yelling for Dame to take off right away. With the banter that goes on between them, it's apparent that all three are acquainted. The former cargo space seats Al in the front, verbally sparring with Dame. Miss Ferns tucks into the space behind Al and tries to secure herself. There are only simple straps to belt them. I climb into my former position in the back, facing rearward with the tail gun. I stow the extra rifle I captured from the first side bin. I've seen lots of occasions in which my sore knuckles would have loved to hold onto a good rifle.

Dame is soon picking up speed down the road. We get airborne and swing toward Nussbaum's train, and he must know things went bad. His train has started moving again. The train alternately stops and starts so often that it might be enough for some people to feel sorry for those poor zombie engineers. Ah well, good exercise for those rigor mortis joints.

*   *   *

Dame questions the rescued pair about Nussbaum's plans. Al explains, "He has the bomb fuel loaded in those tanks on the train. It's a liquid bomb in two parts. Most of it is a powerful acid. As the train rolls through Austren, the liquids inside mix. The volatile component pumps into the acid, quickly heating up and igniting. There is enough there to flatten the town and any nearby hills."

Dame swears, turning the rudder as she adjusts our course. "If that blows up in the capital; there's maybe twenty thousand people living within range of that bomb."

I nod, "And it would throw the territory back into a civil war. That could reignite hostilities between the U.R. and Meztica."

Miss Ferns interrupts, asking the next question on my mind, "Dr. Ehrlichmann, I'm curious about your part in this. Why did you approach the URA?"

"Half of Dr. Nussbaum's inventions are actually mine. When he had trouble with a proper formula, I gave him the breakthrough in the process for turning inmates and the mentally deficient into useful zombie soldiers. The solution is more mine than his."

The way Dr. Al leaned back in his seat and put on a relaxing smile, you'd think he was telling the story to friends over a beer. When his eyes suddenly popped upon and faced Miss Ferns, I think he remembered his audience's background. "Of course, don't tell that in your stories to the public. Dr. Nussbaum is content starting a war trying to control a small part of the world. I, on the other hand, realized the benefits of making a deal with the URA. I will be living in luxury, offering them the latest in biological weapons and chemical agents, enjoying the benefits of a strong nation allied with me. The United Republic will evolve into a new era of military might. I will sit back and reap the benefits while not personally waging any wars."

After listening to the doctor's ramblings, I can't help but weigh in on which man is the bigger danger to the world. Should I worry more about the straightforward-warmonger or the sly snake?

Al's tone abruptly changes as he feels the arc of the plane turning, "What are you doing?"

"Carrying out a bombing run!" Dame shouts.

I suddenly lose sight of the horizon as the nose of the plane dives at its target.

Al begins banging a hand against the plane's fuselage to get Dame's attention. "Wait! Wait! You've got to get me to safety first, then blow up the train!"

I find myself musing how we might use the doctor as a bomb in case the first ones fail. Maybe the hot air inside him or his high ego would be enough to derail the train. My thoughts are interrupted as bullets start peppering the wings and our tub. I glance back in time to see Dame curse. The airplane lurches to the side as more holes appear in the wings. One bomb drops, the other starts to move, but catches and remains under the right wing. That remaining bomb hangs from a single hook cable. As the airplane swerves, I hear the first bomb go off. Feels like one of those peals of thunder shaking every glass in a house. Dame pulls up. Behind us, I see a crater in the earth well off to the side of the rails. The train keeps steaming along. A few more turrets have popped up on top of some of the cars. Soldiers are firing Gatling-type guns back at us.

Al yells out. "You tried to get me killed and you didn't even hit the train!"

I glance back at the same time Dame turns to glare at the doctor. I can see the fresh wound cutting up to a rip in her flight cap. It looks like a shallow bullet nicked her temple. She doesn't say anything, but it seems enough to shut up Al. Dame returns her attention to her airplane and the remaining bomb on the wing.

She studies the wing and declares, "Something is fouled with the release, it won't respond."

Miss Ferns speaks, "Surely there is something we can do. A lot of lives are at stake."

"There is," Dame turns again to stare directly at me. "There's a manual release for letting the bomb loose. Normally it's for taking the bomb off in a hanger. Boxer, you'll have to climb out there and flip the latch when I say."

Just because I climbed outside once, she expects that I'll do it again at her bidding. We're flying barely out of gun range through the morning sky, much faster than any horse, much higher up than any building. I politely decline.

Dame seems upset by my refusal and yells. "You'll do it! You're a natural. I've seen you move along those wing-walker rails. After this I might even book you for a show. It's the only way to drop the bomb and save Austren."

Book me for a show? Is my sarcasm rubbing off on her or is she loaded with enough of her own? I have to admit, when I climbed down earlier, the rails did make things easy. Even so, I still eventually lost my handgrip and fell when I hadn't planned it.

I look at the rails. I glance at the thin wooden wings. I'd love to suggest that she climb out and do it herself, but of course, no one would be flying the airplane. Then I catch a glimpse of Miss Ferns' worry-filled eyes. Something in those eyes makes me want to be a hero.

Despite my better judgment, I start climbing out of my seat. The wind tears at the remains of my damaged suit and stings my eyes. I grab the rail. I remind myself I'd done this once already when I dropped onto the train. At that time we were flying lower, and if I recall correctly, I didn't jump…I fell. My foot finds a spot and pushes forward. Hand over hand, I make slow progress. I edge my way past Miss Fern's admiring eyes. I admit I'm going to develop a fear of beautiful women if just one can encourage me to pull stunts like this without asking. I come upon Al, who is craning his neck over the side to point out positions on the rails. He's giving me thorough insight on where to grab, and what to avoid. I'm tempted to use his throat as a handhold, but it looks too fragile.

I take another step down, but the rail breaks and peels backward. My feet slip as they scrape along the fuselage. My heart leaps into my throat as the airplane seems to accelerate away from me. My hand remains frozen on the bending rail, which snaps backward until it whips me into the tail gun. My body hits the side and I manage to get one foot on a portion of the rail which didn't come loose. I'm temporarily squeezed between the fuselage and the peeled-back railing. My left hand clutches a rod on the rear gun, barely hanging on as I hear Ferns' screams drifting back to me. The rest of the railing drops. It yanks out of my right arm, but I barely manage to catch a new grip on the edge of my sitting-hole. Suddenly I'm petrified with fear. My eyes follow the spinning piece of metal as it falls away.

I realize how lucky I was, not because I held on to the tail gun, but because one finger wrapped into the trigger guard and yet I avoided shooting myself. Hanging against the plane in this position, a sudden let-go would also likely slide me crotch-first into the rudder. Hands shaking, strong winds pulling at me with cold claws, I manage to pull myself back into my seat.

Miss Ferns looks over the side, at the spot where most of the rail once attached. "Oh no more risks like that! We need a new plan."

Al doesn't seem distressed about it. His voice sounds remarkably cheerful as he suggests to Dame, "Emerson, you'll have to go back to the barn. I'll help you get the bombs fixed and maybe you can catch Dr. Nussbaum on the return trip. I'll stay behind to formulate a new plan in case you have trouble finding him after his bomb goes off."

Dame's answer includes new curses I hadn't heard yet. The woman is quite a resource on such expressions. "And by that time, people are going to die! I'm not giving up on this!"

As I listen, my eyes focus on a solution next to me. I hoist the rifle where the rest can see it. "I can shoot the attachment holding the bomb."

The moment I say it, I regret it.

Dame is slow to answer, "It's our only choice. I'm turning for the next run!"

Both occupants in front of me swing worried glances between my position and the bomb under the wing. I can imagine the worst-case scenarios going through their minds at that moment.

The morning sun swings around to a different angle as she lines up the airplane for her approach. I turn and find a position from which I can properly seat the rifle. The train, tracks, hills, and bushes pass below, but my field of view narrows to the iron sights. That hook cable doesn't look as easy a target as when I'd thought up this stupid plan. I breathe. In. Out. I watch how the sights move. The wind doesn't help, and the cable holding up the bomb has a slight swing to it.

"Don't shoot the bomb!" Al yells. Apparently, the doctor thinks I'm dumb enough to not realize this. I'd love to lower the rifle to glare at him, but he is right on one point. I'm dumb enough to point a gun near a bomb.

Bullet sounds start whizzing by us. Dame yells for me to be ready. I take shallow breaths, watching the sights bob a bit with each breath. The creaking cable still swings slightly. I match the timing with my breathing. It's a hard task keeping the rifle lined up in the right place.

A couple rounds from the train jab into *Liberty Flyer*. I see a wood chip fly off the wing near the bomb. I can hear, more than see, Miss Ferns and Al shuffling and straining their safety belts to curl up as small as possible in their seats.

Dame guides us into a slight turn. Everything lines up in front of me for a moment. The tracks align beyond the hook cable, with the steam of the train engine blowing from below us. It isn't a perfect alignment for Dame yet, so she makes another slight turn as enemy fire whizzes past.

"Now!" Dame calls.

My exhale and the cable position coincide to line up the shot. I squeeze off a round. The rifle's noise, smoke, and kick knock my eyes off the target for a moment. My eyes clear even as my brain registers that the bomb hasn't killed me in an explosion. To my dismay, the cable and bomb are still there, which means the rifle sights are off. A slight gap of air left and right of the target makes me wonder which direction the sights have been altered. I don't know which way I missed.

Liberty Flyer is climbing again, as every head in front of me swivels to look at the untouched train below and the bomb still hanging under the wing. Dame smacks her fist against the front of the cockpit, "Well? What happened?"

Over Al and Miss Ferns' similar questions, I shout back, "The sights must be jostled to one side."

Al points at some of the new holes in the airplane. "We can't try that anymore! This is ridiculous!"

"Then the capital and thousands of lives are going to be lost!" Dame argues.

Miss Ferns puts a hand on Al's shoulder. "Doctor, isn't there anything else we can do with that bomb?"

Al starts rattling off a few theories, none of which will help our immediate situation. Most of his thoughts revolve around flying away and trying things after the capital will likely be ruins. I have an idea, but I'm distracted by figuring how badly the sights are off. I need to know where the bullet is going, at a distance similar to where the hook cable sits. I aim at a chipped paint spot on the wing, breathe out, and pull the trigger.

That puts a sudden halt to everyone's discussion. No one misses the fact that I intentionally put another bullet hole into the wing.

Dame points it out with her middle finger and yells. "For every hole you put in my baby I'm going to put one in your hide! Are you trying to set off the bomb and kill us in the air?"

I keep staring down the sights at the hole I just made and now I know how to adjust my aim. Hitting that cable should be a lot easier, though still difficult. Dame is still yelling her own train of obscenities. Much as I alternately love and hate her attitudes, it's shameful fun to put a burr under her seat.

"Relax," I say. "I figured out the sights. We should do fine."

"Fine?!" Al sputters, "We can't dive over that train again! Their guns will rake me apart!"

I shake my head, "We don't have to fly over it."

I point out to the side. Nussbaum's train is moving parallel with us, though Dame is keeping out of range of their guns. Once again, I can clearly see the odd outline of the engine. It's built to take punishment. The engine's body hides within that snow-plow shape designed for colder climates. The hardened steel plates on the outside are angled to throw snow up and out, and for all I know might be capable of deflecting a bomb.

"That engine is a tough nut to crack and protected by guns." My pointing finger sweeps forward. "So why not bomb the track? It may not put an end to our evil friend, but whether you hit the train or the rails, the train won't deliver its bomb. That's the mission, right?" Heads nod in agreement. "So, let's just fly a little ahead of the train and blow the tracks."

Now that we have a sound plan that doesn't include flying close enough to get shot up, everyone's attitudes improve. That good feeling only lasts until I start aiming the rifle at the bomb. From the corner of my eyes I can see the track passing closer and closer. The train engine isn't very far behind us and I can hear some kind of whistle signal, probably for the rooftop gunmen. A moment later, bullets fly around us again, though not as often nor accurately as before. Dame keeps the airplane flying more evenly than the first passes mover the train. I time my breathing with the sway of the cable holding the bomb. Feels like everything we'd worked for sits on my shoulders. At any moment those rails would be right below us.

Dame calls the command. I don't hurry the shot, using only a fraction of a second to match my breathing to the cable. The rifle spits and bucks. As soon as Dame hears the sound, she pulls up hard to get us away from the explosion. It was well that she did. As I quickly turn to the rear and drop into my seat, I see the bomb fall. I catch a glimpse of the menacingly-sloped engine before the earth flies into the sky between us. A thunderous clamor hammers the airplane and sets our ears ringing. *Liberty Flyer* rattles. Despite Dame's last-second ascent, the proximity of the blast still showers us with mud and strips some paint off the fuselage.

Dr. Nussbaum's train begins hissing steam and clanging a bell. The brakes start squealing. Through the rain of rocks, I can see the tracks interrupted by a crater capable of swallowing a building. I shout at the poor zombie engineers, "Time to stop the train for good!"

Their own momentum proves too great. Without really slowing, the front wheels of the engine launch into empty air. The nose tips down. The sloped plow design slams into the opposite wall of the crater, followed by tons of speeding metal wedging it further into the earth. Dozens of heavy train cars slam and push into the back of that stuck engine. With the nose trapped, the tail end of the engine is shoved upward. The rest of the train bunches up behind it. The air fills with the sounds of tearing and groaning metal. The rest of the train derails or crunches together like an accordion. Cars veer off the tracks left and right. Some roll over. My attention is on those first few cars following the engine; they continue to wedge under its back end, further lifting the engine tail. In moments, I see something I never would have imagined: an engine rising upright on its nose. As all of us watch with gaping mouths as the engine continues tumbling forward. Flipping back end over front, the train falls onto its roof. Within seconds the boiler explodes and hot steam escapes. Torn metal and ignited ammo blow skyward.

No one says anything for the longest time. Dame banks into a full circle. From a safe distance, we watch the separated train shudder to a stop. A few brush fires start and add to the smoke plume from the unraveled engine. No guns fire. We only hear our own propeller and the squeals of tortured metal from the ground. A few cars remain untouched and upright, though unable to go anywhere on their own, exactly like we wanted.

The doctor observes, "It's a good thing those tanker cars at the back didn't have a worse collision. If those had mixed, we'd be looking at a valley instead of a train." The doctor is smiling down at the wreckage. His hands give the kind of short clapping reserved for someone's horse getting a third-place prize. "At least this way, maybe Nut Tree survived. I'll still have a chance to make him my personal servant zombie."

His words seem to remind everyone that it may not be safe to remain in the area. The train is history and Nussbaum can't threaten the capital, so our part is done. After a quick discussion, we agree to fly to the capital and let Governor Torres know where he can send the army to pick up whatever is left of Nussbaum.

*   *   *

Austren, the capital of Texico, is much bigger and more impressive than one would expect in this cactus countryside. Moments after Dame landed, some of Torres' local badges tucked the airplane into hiding in a warehouse. Someone must have wired our arrival to the governor because he and some URA suits I didn't know arrive before the sun passes the midpoint of the sky. Governor Torres' caravan of carriages appears escorted by a cavalry unit.

No one needs to point out Torres to me. The Meztican-born, former general practically jumps out of the carriage and strides toward us like a soldier on a mission. His suit isn't any uniform: black coattails, red cumber bun, slicked-back hair and polished leather shoes. Despite his formal attire, his deeply-tanned skin is thick and wrinkled like leather, and when I shake his hand the callouses are noticeable. He eyes us like a hawk would. Most important, a sidearm strapped to his leg that looks more practical than ornamental. All in all, I'd say someone tried to dress a bulldog up like a peacock.

"I'm Governor Torres," He jabs one finger at us while the other hand rests on the butt of his pistol. "I need to know who the devil you are and where is Nussbaum? I have a train full of staff ready to evacuate, and I need to know if I should be running back there right now."

I'm wondering if he has similar plans to evacuate thousands of innocent people. I'm in no hurry to speak up. Thankfully, someone else jumps to the fore. Al jumps forward with a handshake extended, but the governor never removes his right hand from his sidearm. The doctor retracts his hand and speaks without any apparent curbing of enthusiasm.

"I am Doctor Ehrlichmann, we've corresponded but never met."

There's a glint in Torres' eyes when he hears the name. I have trouble translating his body language. It either 'he needs to be my new best friend' or 'here's someone I need to exploit.'

Ehrlichmann continues, offhandedly waving an arm at the rest of us. "These are my associates. I have great news! We delivered some bombs of my own making and blew Nussbaum off his tracks. His train is scattered in disarray across the desert. This cavalry should have no problem rounding them up."

The governor narrowed his eyes at the doctor, not the expression Al hoped to receive.

Torres barked, "Nussbaum isn't dead?!"

The doctor sighs and his hand waves back to indicate Dame and I. "They can explain it better."

The foremost thought on my mind is that weasel forgot that our original orders would have put an end to both him and Nussbaum with his own bombs. There had been no rescue involved with that course.

Facing down Torres, I spoke calmly. "The train was armored and protected by a half dozen machine gun turrets. Have a look at the damage to the plane." I jerked my thumb over my shoulder, pointing at the warehouse. "Dropping a bomb on the tracks was the best we could do. It stopped him from reaching Austren."

The governor stared us down. A camera flash caught our attention. Only then did I realize Miss Ferns had slipped away from our sides and set herself apart. Her camera snapped a second picture as Governor Torres softened his look.

"This is good news!" She exclaimed. Somehow, that lady always seemed to find enthusiasm at the oddest moments. "The people have been saved from that madman!"

I notice a few of the unknown URA suits nodding, one even whispers words in Torres' ear. Torres drops his tough-guy persona on cue, addressi9ng everyone nearby with a smile. "Indeed. The threat is ended. This will change my statement that was scheduled for this afternoon. We'll inform the good people how my people took care of this threat. It's only right to set their minds at ease."

The governor motions the doctor and the reporter toward his carriage. "Doctor, I'd like to catch up on our acquaintance a bit. Young reporter, you may join us and I'll get you to the planned press meeting."

Governor Torres didn't immediately follow them. As the doctor and reporter boarded his carriage, he spun back on me and Dame.

The smile was gone. "I'm glad to see Ehrlitch? Dr Lickman? Dr You-Know-Who over there!"

I worked hard to maintain a straight face.

Torres, however, was not in a good mood and his angry tone continued without a beat, "But I know the pilot had orders to bomb that train out of existence. Now I've still got a madman assassin out there gunning for ME!."

Dame took more heat from that look than I did. Her grease-stained clothes and flying goggles identified her as the pilot.

He spoke low and slow, making sure we didn't miss a word of what came next. "We're going to a public address. You'll get recognized as my specialists who took down this threat on my orders. After that, you aren't going anywhere. I'll want that plane back in the air and helping the ground troops track down that snake. Are we clear?"

We both nodded. Satisfied, he spun back to his carriage and left us standing there.

The URA suits debrief us further and take our news with mixed enthusiasm. Like Torres, they're glad the bomb threat was eliminated, but they don't appreciate having to go out and hunt down their vilified scientist. I overheard one dictating a telegram message for his bosses, claiming it as a victory even though the same guy just grilled me for my incompetence. Funny how government officials can take good news and make it sound like you should have done much better, then turn around and report to others about a good job accomplished as if they'd carried out the job themselves.

That's what ends up happening. Governor Torres had a statement scheduled with the press and some officials that afternoon. We stand present, though we're off to the side and somewhat hidden. He doesn't plan on making our names known or giving us any attention. Torres notifies the press (which included Miss Ferns, but no other women) about Dr. Nussbaum's failed attack. Torres takes most of the credit, claiming he sent his best regiment to take care of the problem. At least Al gets a moment of recognition, but before the doctor can even speak, Torres ropes the audience back into his own grandeur. As the speech wears on, I fight the fatigue of standing upright.

Things get interesting when some odd craft appears in the sky on the horizon. I stare at it for a bit, trying to decide what it is. Others start noticing it too, though Torres continues his grand speech. As it gets closer, more folks realize something is wrong and begin whispering as they stare. A number of journalists turn to snap photos of the flying contraption. I'm just starting to realize that the object in the sky is much larger than *Liberty Flyer*, and it's unlike anything I've ever seen. It seems to be some kind of balloon. There's a cloth-like tarp bubbled over the top, shimmering as the air currents blow past. The base of the balloon seems to be composed of several objects, some boxy, and others oval like a pill. Extending out in six directions are arms connecting to six individual propellers. Each propeller is facing into the sky, sweeping air below the craft to help guide it and keep it aloft.

Al is standing right next to me, but his eyes are closed. I nudge him harder-than-necessary with an elbow and jerk a thumb to the sky. "What's that?"

His eyes take a moment to focus, before gasping, "He actually followed my suggestion! I gave designs to Dr. Nussbaum a year ago showing how he could merge his dirigible with some of his train cars." His eyebrows lower as he glares at it. "It just means Nut Tree is stealing my ideas once again. That's my creation! And he's sitting in it, stealing my glory!"

Dame is on the other side of the doctor; she's glaring as much as I am at our self-centered brainchild. Miss Ferns appears at our side as well.

I interrupt Al's tirade. "So you knew he had a chance to turn his train into a flying machine?! Do you suppose he also rigged a way to carry the bomb inside that thing?"

Al flippantly replies, "Oh, of course! With my designs he could easily…" The doctor stops and his eyes go wide as he finally catches up to the implications.

Now that he's said it, I realize the rectangular boxes at the base of the balloon are train cars. A couple of tankers are present. I can't imagine how any kind of balloon could lift them, but I suppose the six upright propellers help.

Governor Torres finally falters in delivering his speech while everyone looks toward the menacing balloon anyway.

A voice carries on the wind. "I've trapped you governor! You couldn't foil destiny…"

Dr. Nussbaum seems to be gloating. His voice cackles from some kind of amplifier. He delivers a threatening message to the governor and people of Texico. You can feel the glee in his voice as he presses on to carry out his mad plan despite the setbacks we gave him.

Although, as far as his exact words go, I can't understand more than a handful of them. His message is too far away and he sounds like he's spitting into the sound device. We do hear his laughter clearly enough. The rest doesn't really matter. The sight of this frightening thing looming in the sky is enough to cause panic. Folks scatter in every direction.

Not to be deterred, Al jumps past the governor to the now-abandoned podium and speaker. He glares towards Nussbaum's vehicle. "We will have the last laugh! You've benefited from my theorems, my formulae, you took my suggestions…all of my work without sharing due credit! I will send up a plane to stop you. My minions will rip you out of the sky."

Al turns around to see Dame and I glaring; even Miss Ferns looks cross. He continues to look pompous as he offers, "When I say 'my minions' I mean it with the utmost respect."

Dame turns and sprints toward the warehouse hiding her airplane. To my surprise and her credit, Miss Ferns follows. Al looks like he's about to cheer us on, which stops abruptly as I lay one of my hands on his coat. I growl, "We're all catching this flight."

If we're about to get killed in the air chasing a madman, I'll be happy having Dr. Honest Man dying by my side. Of course, he begins to protest. I simply throw him over my shoulder and run.

*   *   *

We get to the warehouse as a few guards are rolling Dame's wounded bird onto a straight gravel road. She is at the controls, cranking the hesitant propeller. Miss Ferns, riding in the cargo space, waves at us. I feel almost sorry to dump our spindly professor next to her. I jump into the rear seat. Dame yells back a few pointers about the tail gun, reiterating that I'm not to put any more bullet holes in her aircraft that I wouldn't put in my own hide. The sound of several safety tethers latching is almost simultaneous as the plane lines up for takeoff. The engine comes to life. Gears and belts begin spinning as the propeller whirs faster than the eyes can track. A burst of oily smoke blows past us to the rear. The ground helpers take that as their cue to run for their lives. *Liberty Flyer* roars down the road and catches the wind. Dame noses her craft upward as I stare down behind us. On the ground, I see the toppled podium outside the governor's office surrounded by abandoned papers and tipped-over seats. The only people I can see outside are mounted on horses and fleeing Austren as fast as they can gallop.

I glance back over my shoulder. Both Miss Ferns and Al are nervous. Ferns has her camera ready, but her hands are a little shaky. I suppose the doctor feels safer in the plane than on the ground, but his eyes keep looking wistfully north, his best escape route. I imagine they don't feel as if they'd really be of much help, since Dame and I will be firing all the guns.

Since the balloon is still in the distance, I ask the doctor a question that bugged me earlier. "Form-you-lay?"

His eyes are on his mentor's vehicle. "Yes, what of them?"

"What is form-you-lay?"

He glances back at me as if I dropped out of grade school. "F-o-r-m-u-l-a-e. The plural of formula. He stole several of mine."

"Oh, formulas."

He shakes his head, "No, no. Formulae. It's from the old language."

I shrug, "Why not just say formulas, it's easier."

"I don't have time to educate simpletons!"

Dame shouts, "Just shut up! A couple things just dropped off the balloon!"

"Dirigible!" Al argues.

At least my plan worked. I find I'm more relaxed for having hassled him and even Miss Ferns is cracking a smile.

I try to see what Dame is concerned about, but at the moment my view is blocked. Al is leaning over a bit to look under us. "It's Nussbaum's fighter planes." He calmly explains, though the news brings our anxiety back to the fore. "I borrowed some of their designs to give some improvements to Jane Emerson," he uses his thumb to point to Dame, "for this airplane. His fighters are actually pretty small."

"And more maneuverable!" Dame yells, interspersed with more curses.

I'd love to strangle Doctor Al for his lack of warnings about Nussbaum's toys, but I don't have time.

Liberty Flyer turns one way then the next. The horizon tilts and spins a bit as I try not to lose my stomach. I hear bullets whiz nearby. Dame's Gatlings are keeping busy. I'm looking up at the ground as few brass casings spin in the air over my head. We right ourselves with the horizon as a shadow passes. One of the 'fighter planes' pops into my view.

Liberty Flyer looks like she's a fat hen compared to the scrawny, skeletal, framework sparrows chasing her. The fighter has no side panels to cover up the engine or the pilot. The smaller craft has a similar stick-and-canvas framework similar to that Wright Brothers' plane I saw in the newspapers years back. Their exposed engines seem to make all the difference. Even then, I doubt it's capable of carrying more than one person or gun. The first one is gone from my sight before I can even line up a shot.

Dame's voice is nearly lost on the wind, but it still gives me fair warning. A second airplane pops into view. I throw my arms and weight into the gun, cranking out bullets and turning to match the enemy. He dips out of view, likely unhurt but at least I turned him off course. In the next second, Dame rolls the airplane and he pops back into my sights. I crank several more rounds into the sky before losing sight of him again.

In the course of Dame's turn, I find I'm staring at Nussbaum's dirbel…dirigibly…damn balloon again. I turn and yell at Dame, but I doubt my words can reach her. Miss Ferns listens to me, even as she's gripping a rail with white knuckles.

"Dame just needs to head straight for the balloon and take it out! I'll keep them off our back!"

As I turn my attention to the tail, the word passes forward from mouth to mouth. The world tilts again as we change direction. I have a brief opening at one enemy, sending a few rounds his way before he goes farther than I can rotate. I hear his gun spitting back at us, but I don't think he hit anything.

I chance a look over my shoulder. We're getting closer to the balloon. Al turns his head to me and hollers. "Dame counts only two enemy airplanes!"

I nod and turn back, only in time to see one diving down at us. He's shooting, I'm shooting, Dame is shooting. A couple rounds punch into the tail, while I drill a few through his wings. The enemy drops below us, yet a moment later more rounds are zipping past our heads originating from the balloon. From the chorus of our crew's shouts, I deduce the railway cars under the balloon still have some machine gun mounts operating. Dame stops firing and we bank upward at a sharp angle. I hear Al saying something about getting above the dirgybell's cover. As we climb, my view allows me to see the second fighter lurking behind. I manage only one round before the magazine empties.

The second fighter climbs and fires. He's slowly gaining. Unlike Dame's guns, which have a machine that unloads and loads the next clip for her, I have to manhandle this thing off and replace it with one tucked in a closed box at my feet. I no sooner get it unattached before the next fighter draws closer, bullets whining right by me. He's close enough for me to clearly make out his zombie gas mask and goggles. To Hell with how Dame feels about my next action: I haul back and chuck the empty magazine at the other guy. It glances off a wing and bounces into his framework fuselage. He breaks off his attack without actually suffering too much damage. Too bad I didn't knock his head off. By the time Dame has leveled out above the height of the balloon, I've managed to plant the next magazine in place.

I hear Miss Ferns praising Dame. "You got one bellowing smoke!"

Since there is no smoke behind us, I assume she means one of the six propellers. We turn to line up for Dame's next attack. Dr. Nussbaum's voice is in the air once again, directing some message out of his speakers. As far as I'm concerned, he's wasting his breath. With all the noise and wind I can't tell what he's saying, and what I'm able to hear sounds like he's still spitting all over the device.

My stomach's lighter and I'm staring up into only blue sky. Dame's flying closer to the speaker. Her guns drum to life again. Nussbaum's speaker cuts out in a loud squawk. A rain of bullet casings spin past my head. She uses up the entire twin magazines before pulling back hard. Sky is replaced by the ground again as she pulls out of the dive. We dip into the balloon's field of fire. Train-mounted machine guns blaze for a few frightening heartbeats as we climb back to safety. I catch sight of two smoking propellers extending from the balloon. One of them explodes.

We're climbing and two airplanes are following. One is too far away to be effective; the other is sending bullets over my head. He's close enough to do some real damage soon. He's also flying right where I can't possibly miss.

I smirk, "Here's your bye-bye kiss, baby."

I pound his airplane with hammering bullets. Smoke and sparks pop from the engine. I see the zombie pilot's body twitch as holes appear on his jacket. The bullets in his body don't cause him much concern. His airplane proves to be less durable. The engine flares into a fiery comet. He spins beneath my sight. Looks like it will be a nice meteor shower in store for Austren. I send a few rounds at the other airplane, but Dame once again levels out and banks for another attack, so I lose him.

Dame swears. "I've used up all my bullets! I've got nothing left!"

Turns out the last magazines to be cycled into place were empty ones from earlier. I turn to glance at them, just in time for some hot oil to sprinkle my cheek and shoulder. There's smoke coming from our own engine, and I don't need to guess where the spraying oil originated.

I shout, "I took out one of the zombie fighters, but there's still another one behind us."

As soon as I've said it, Al perks up. "The pilots are zombies too? Why didn't you tell me?" He unfastens his safety latch. "Fly straight so it can get close behind us. Don't shoot it."

Dame holds our course. Before long, the other pilot is up and behind us. I lean over the gun and sight him, just in case. "Careful!" Miss Ferns grumbles as the spindly doctor climbs over her.

Al yells at me, "Give me a moment!"

On the tail rudder, I see the reflection of flashing lights. Al is holding his pen, except it isn't a pen. He continues to flash a sequence of lights from the tip, alternating between red and green. The zombie pilot flies steady. I could probably put one through his head, and he could certainly rake us with bullets if he wanted. I hold my fire and so does he. Al sits down. The enemy pilot just follows us at a leisurely cruise.

"And he's mine!" Al proclaims, buckling back into his seat. "He's in 'lemming' mode. He'll follow me regardless of his own safety. I'm his master now!" Cue the madman cackle, which Al performs flawlessly.

"And now what?" Miss Ferns asks.

"I don't know, but at least I reclaimed the first of many." The doctor shrugs. "We've done our best. It's probably better if we fly away from the blast area. I'll have to make a few more zombies and come back to catch Nut Tree."

It's sickening how calmly he refers to a city full of people simply as 'the blast area.'

Dame points at the other plane. "Can't you order him to attack?"

Al is shaking his head. "It's not that precise, I have to be able to talk to him. I wouldn't anyway; I appreciate finally having one back under my command."

Dame banks around. We all watch Nussbaum's balloon as it limps along on four engines. It's still drawing determinedly closer to the fringe of Austren. *Liberty Flyer* sputters a moment, sending more smoke trailing behind us.

An idea hits. I turn to yell at Dame. "Dame?"

Somehow, its quiet enough now that she can hear me. "Yeah, Boxer?"

I point to the airplane behind us. "He's a 'lemming' right now! He'll follow you wherever you fly regardless of danger! I imagine he's full of fuel!"

Dame understands. She starts turning toward the balloon. Al, who hasn't comprehended the plan yet, glances back at me with a worried look on his face. "Does this mean we might be flying back toward the machine guns?"

I half turn in my seat and give him the friendliest grin yet, "Quite likely!"

We're pointed straight at Nussbaum's flying terror. The zombie flier is following us like the obedient and clueless little puppy. I think I know how Miss Ferns and Al felt when we last took off—that I'm not in control and just along for the ride at this point. A last glance toward the front and I see Dame beginning to dive, outlined against the much larger balloon.

I sit down, keeping my head low as I resume my watch to the rear. Bullets start zipping past us. I hear one strike somewhere, followed by the sight of a few glints of debris spraying out. A metallic clank hits somewhere under my seat. Al shouts something that is lost in the noise. Miss Ferns screams. I see a chip of wood fly off the tail. Several more bullets can be heard whizzing past.

The extended propeller arms of the balloon come into view. The other plane is still well above us, trying to follow in a dive. I see him clip one of the balloon's untouched propellers. The propeller blades shred and the lemming plane starts to spin and fly apart. We pass under the balloon so closely that it feels as if I could stick a bat or umbrella up in the air and touch the underside of the train cars. The sound of the fighter's collision assaults my ears like one of Al's bombs went off. Pieces of debris are blown out, raining down behind our tail. I want to scream at Dame to fly faster, but I hear our engine sputtering. We bolt out from under the far side of the balloon.

A pair of gun turrets stares at me from the train cars. I lean forward and crank out my last few rounds. The other guns fire back; one shot manages to strike a spark off the side of my gun. Smoke from our own engine begins to cloud my vision.

Even though we're still too close to the enemy guns, an explosion rips through the balloon above them. Flames begin devouring the air-filled fabric. The guns fall silent as the hungry fire spreads. I have a feeling we've finally struck a mortal blow to Nussbaum's doomsday transport. Unfortunately, the smoke from our own stuttering engine worries me more.

Oil sprays across one wing. Even more worrisome, the propeller jerks to a sudden stop. I barely see an outline of Dame due to the smoke pouring from the front. Al is dabbing a pocket handkerchief over blood on his arm. Miss Ferns is looking over my shoulder, taking a picture of the other doctor's fiery contraption. This time, a normal flash comes out.

"Dame? Can you hear me?"

She's moving but not responding, or if she is responding, I can't hear it. Through the sideboards I can feel her hitting or kicking something. The propellers remain frozen. The doctor turns and reaches a hand to Dame. He starts to say something, but he recoils his hand and his sentence dies out. There is blood on his hand that wasn't there before. Dame's blood. It's spilling from a hole in her leather jacket, behind her right shoulder. It's the arm she uses to fly the airplane.

All we can do is look backward and forward, assessing the outcome in the relative quiet of the wind. Nut Tree's balloon is losing altitude even faster than its shape. A raging fire belches from the middle. One train car rips partway loose, hangs for a moment, and then plunges hundreds of feet to the ground. Another propeller explodes, raining debris. We're dropping too, albeit gliding along the currents. Our engine seems beyond hope. I'd actually feel better if Dame cursed; instead, she's quietly fighting the stick with both hands to guide us down gently. An eternity of seconds tick by as the ground rises. I see Dame's head slowly dip, only to jerk upright again. She's fighting to stay conscious and in control. The three of us behind Dame start to panic for more reasons than the rising ground.

As Dame fought to stay conscious, we've drifted a slow circle just in time to crash in roughly the same area as the evil doctor's transport. It's the last place we want to be! A mass of flaming tarp, train cars and propeller arms skids into the ground perpendicular to our path. It's the second spill of train cars I've seen today. Tankers rip apart and liquid belches from them.

Al cries out and ducks lower into his seat. I recall the bomb was made of a mix of two liquids, one of them a powerful acid. A sizzling, bubbling lake of fluid is filling a depression just ahead of our path. All three of us are yelling at Dame, but I don't think she can hear us. I doubt Dame can do much else to avert a crash.

The fiery balloon fabric tears free of the remainder of the train. It floats and rolls on the wind currents out of our way. Left behind, the heavy train cars and splintered propeller arms slide to a stop.

Dame makes a last effort to turn us away as I hear the wheels clipping the cacti.

We hit the ground. The restraint latches keep me seated, at the expense of some bruises. The airplane jolts one way and the next as we lose our wheels. I watch one whole wing blow over me and get left behind. Dust and smoke obscure everything else. It shudders to a stop as pieces of the wing frame collapses.

I'm amazed we're alive. The airplane stopped, partly leaning to one side. There have been times when I've been bruised worse, but I've always had time to recover. Despite pain in my shoulders and back, I start throwing loose my restraint latch. I hop out as Al and Miss Ferns are doing the same. The lake of acid bubbles is not far away, but it's not coming any closer. The doctor goes over to get a closer look at it. Miss Ferns and I share a different concern: our pilot.

Dame's oil-covered face is whispering as she pats the dashboard dials, "I knew you'd help us down in one piece. Stalwart and graceful in life and death."

Miss Ferns helps me remove Dame's latches. I realize I should stop using the nickname I gave her back when I thought she was just another URA stooge. Jane Emerson has earned my respect. I hesitate to move her, but the engine has fire smoke rising from it. My best grip is to get under her shoulders with my arms and push my feet against a wing. She screams at first. With some effort, I get her to the ground. I find a first aid box next to the seat and ask Miss Ferns to pull it free.

Miss Ferns comforts Jane. "Hang in there. I'm getting Mr. Boxer some bandages. We'll patch you up and get help in Austren."

Jane winces as I start bandaging her, but she forces a smile. I don't think I've seen her smile before now. She hisses a reply as I finish the bandage. She even jokes, "Just make sure you tell them alcohol cleans a wound inside and out. Lots of it!"

Jane seems fine. We leave her comfortable in the shadow of a wing and walk over to see what the doctor is doing. Our crash site is on a gently sloping hill supporting cacti and scrub brush. The slope is interrupted by a line of half-buried boulders downhill from us. Al is standing on a large boulder at the edge of the new acid lake. Upon seeing our approach, he gestures excitedly down toward the wreckage sizzling in the middle.

"We're very lucky. The detonation chemical remains safely contained in that oil car." He's pointing at one with white and red markings. It sits on top of the wreckage of some other cars. "If that one had leaked into the acid, we'd be dead before the folks on the far side of Austren heard the explosion."

Miss Ferns and I exchange nervous glances. I suggest, "We may want to move away from here while we can. We should get our pilot to town."

"No one is going anywhere!" A voice shouts from above.

It's Dr. Nussbaum. He's in the air, gliding down to us. On his back is a contraption that hisses jets of steam toward the ground. In one hand he's holding some odd gun pointed at us. Coils of tubes connect it to the jet backpack. He lands on the boulder next to us. He's slightly above us, and would likely take me four long seconds to run and jump over to his spot. As I'm wondering what kind of gun he's holding, I realize mine is still holstered. I think he sees my hand twitch closer to it.

"One move and we all die," he declares, holding up a box with wires sticking out of one end. "With this detonator, I can still cause the chemical to spray out of the connector. When that happens, they will have to scrape our bodies from the moon!"

The doctor is watching us all too closely. I won't be able to get my gun out in time, and I'm too far away to rush him with my knuckles, *if* I can slip those into place.

Al takes center stage. "And if we die, know that I foiled your plans! You couldn't stage a successful war without my help, and you can't even set off a bomb without me."

The two rivals bicker at each other. I watch closely at every twitch of Nussbaum's gun, awaiting a proper opportunity.

Nussbaum's gun swivels toward Al's head. "Dr. Ehrlichmann, how you disappoint me! My star pupil, reducing himself to a government lackey! You are just a lapdog for the URA!"

"Dr. Nussbaum, you trudged into dangerous decisions before me! You made enemies of those who wielded governing power! The resources of the URA would have been better used aiding us than against us! The URA would have picked supporting our scientific progress and military inventions over that charismatic soldier Torres if you had played your test tubes in the right order! They could just as easily have made *him* the bad guy and exonerated us as heroes of the war!"

Nusbaum fumed, his gun still pointing at Al. "You deserve to be a zombie along with those other disappointments who once thought to help me. I should have given *you* the endotracheal insertion you demanded!"

"Ha! You would have likely messed up the process! Your only hope would have been to research the formulas…bah, *formulae* you stole from me!"

At Al's slip of the tongue on "formulas," he can't help but glance in disdain at the one whose conversation from earlier must have tripped him up. His eyes widen as he sees my barrel pointing at Nussbaum. Now

Al can't take his eyes off me and his old teacher is a second from realizing his fatal error. My sights are lined up on Nusbaum's head.

Click!

I guess I'm an idiot for forgetting to reload my gun after a morning of shooting zombies.

Al rolls his eyes up at the sky. Nussbaum looks at me with astonishment. Whether he is more surprised that I almost had him or that I bungled the attempt is hard to judge. A smile slowly lifts the corners of Nussbaum's wrinkly face. His gun rises in my direction.

Boom!

The loud sound I'd heard on the train last night goes off next to me. Like paper bits blown out of a cannon, pieces of Nussbaum scatter into the air over the acid lake. Bits of hair, a dismembered shoe, the gun, a few pencils and gobs of pink and red rain down into the bubbling fluid. The steaming jet backpack hisses in an erratic aerial dance before splashing to its doom.

I turn around to witness that Miss Ferns has once again been knocked on her butt. It had to be the recoil. The smoking, two-shot, Al-modified pistol is in her hand. She sheepishly looks from her gun to me and says, "I still had one left."

That gun must have been what knocked the hole in the wall of the train car that morning during the moment I'd looked away. I offer a hand down to my rescuer. She accepts with flushed cheeks as she gets back on her feet. I'm amused and grateful I wasn't the only one who drew their gun while the doctors were occupied.

Al's spindly limbs go into a little dance as he whoops and hollers. "I'm so glad he found his demise facing one of my inventions!"

Miss Ferns and I share a smile at over her resourcefulness and our survival. Heedless, Al keeps on skipping and preaching. "Now things can finally move forward! Oh, I wish I could have taken him alive. He would have become the prototype of my new version of fearless soldiers."

We both lose our smile. Miss Ferns asks, "A prototype?"

"Oh yes! Nut Tree left a lot of room for improvement. There's no shortage of killers and rapists in prisons in the United Republic! I'll convert the first to regular undead soldiers. Others I can make into walking bombs. Or maybe, oh yes, I can use steam-jet packs! Make them into living bombs and have them fly to a target. Haha, I will call it a 'smart' bomb! Ooh! Even more insidious and effective: plague-bearers. The first ones start spreading disease in an enemy's civilian centers. Later ones can walk in and lay claim to the cities, perform a clean-up, with no effect on themselves."

I'm becoming horrified at the picture Al's painting of future warfare. A glance at Miss Ferns reassures me that someone else shares my feelings. She can normally hold a disarming smile through anything, but her eyes are wide and her fingers are covering her dropped jaw. The doctor continues to ramble on as he struts at the edge of the raised rocks, just above eddies of sizzling acid. My hand goes into my pocket and settles into the reassuring weight of the personalized brass knuckles purely out of habit. My vision darts between the lake of acid and the madman strutting perilously close to it.

I've done my job for the URA and the people of Austren. Yet, I wonder if I've saved their fate if men like this have their twisted ambitions funded by the government. The suits will love having Dr. Ehrlichmann in their corner. Do I really want to deliver a knockout punch that sends a man into acid, just for what he might do? On the other hand, I feel pretty sure the world might be a happier place without such men. I sometimes find it hard to fight temptation, and even Pops and Dongel know how unpredictable I can be with some of their orders. I've already clenched and re-clenched my fist around the reliable knuckles six or eight times.

It dawns on me. Let the choice be Al's. With my other hand, I fish a coin out of my pocket. I hold it up for him. He stops his dance and looks at it. "Call it in the air."

I send it spinning upward. He doesn't even ask about the prize of the bet, although it will likely affect all of Texico territory. Al points at his glorious brain and declares, "I always bet heads!"

The coin descends into my hand. I slap it onto my other arm. I don't think Al has noticed the brass knuckles adorning it. I lift my hand to reveal the coin and glance at Miss Ferns. She looks at me hard and nods.

About the Author…

Douglas was born Nov 28th, 1971. He got the chance to live in many different places while growing up, courtesy of the assignments the US Army offered his father. Quiet and shy, he dreamed of other worlds and places…and desired to write about them. He got into fantasy role-playing games in his mid-teens. To this day he regularly meets friends in tabletop role-playing games and online adventures. Many of his characters evolved in games, and each developed their own personality.

Having to rely on self-publishing for his novels, Douglas was surprised at the amount of good reviews and publicity they received. The *Earthrin Stones* trilogy sold more copies than expected. *The Widow Brigade* started its reception earning ten straight 5-star reviews, including a recent widow who said it helped with her healing process.

Though Douglas expanded his entertaining to include game streams and recordings on YouTube and Twitch, his passion remains centered on his writing.

Douglas lives with his wife and two sons in Minnesota. He works in health care, serving people's needs in medical imaging. When most people see him, he is wearing scrubs.

Learn more about the author and the Realm of Dhea Loral at…
Website – DheaLoral.com
Facebook – Dhea Loral
Twitter - @ThaminDheaLoral
YouTube - Thamin DheaLoral
Twitch: - Thamin_T

About the Editor

Denise Guibord is a freelance editor and writer who loves the creative process in nearly all crafts from writing to knitting to painting. As an editor, she works with authors to tighten up scenes and descriptions, smooth out punctuation and mechanics, and guide the project to bridge its layers of connecting details, all while honoring the author's original voice and intention. Her website is www.deniseguibord.com

Want to experience more of the world of Dhea Loral? Explore the dwarf homelands through the eyes of revolutionary Duli! *The Widow Brigade* opened on Amazon with seven critiques praising the story, and each giving it a perfect 5 stars! This story features strong women, in a fantasy setting, rebelling against the traditions of a male-dominated society.

"I felt the plot was well developed, well-paced, and the motivations of the characters really drew me in, caring about what happened as the plot progressed. I felt the main character was not your typical shiny hero, or dastardly anti-hero. She just felt real. I highly recommend this book..." - Tom H

"This book is very well written and as always with his stories, the battle scenes are intense, with details that pull you in and fully immerse yourself in the story. The characters are well developed and allow you to enjoy loving and hating them." – Lockhart

Discover the series which introduced fantasy readers to the realm of Dhea Loral. The *Earthrin Stones* trilogy gives the reader the largest backstory and plot driving the scenes of this world. Open your adventure with *Inheritance of a Sword and a Path*!

"Over a thousand years ago the Godswars ravaged the land of Dhea Loral, shattering continents, laying waste to cities, and driving species to extinction. The people of the land are once again starting to prosper and flourish, while the gods stay aloft and watch from afar the recovery. Yet, not all the old quarrels have been forgotten. For some gods, the time is right to once again meddle in the affairs of mortals. Though the gods have bound themselves by a Covenant that bars their direct entry into Dhea Loral, they are able to send mortal emissaries to carry out their schemes."

"*Inheritance of a Sword and a Path* is a treasure trove of fantasy, eye-popping adventures, lead characters imbued with morality, humility, strength and humor…This saga opener had me turning pages, reading way (way) past my bedtime, and definitely curious for the next installment. Pure fun!" — Lori Crever "30 Minutes with the Author"

Strangers thrown together, forced into service on a common quest, form a bond of camaraderie. Each seeks to find their focus in the world, amidst their private mysteries.

The half-orc savage, who takes pride in a company he no longer serves. The dusk-skinned archer, carrying a bow from her forgotten homeland. The dwarf who studies the past so he can create a future. The knight who pays fealty to no lord. The elf sorceress seeking knowledge, but what specific question is she trying to answer?

They will band together, seeking separate goals. How far will pilgrims travel to discover who they are?

-Pilgrims with Blades: Pressed into Service-

Facing a crisis and looking for any excuse to strike in force against the orcs occupying the hills to their south, the city-state Kashmer conscripts privateers and adventurers into war. A band of strangers must learn to support and adapt to each other as a daring plan separates them from the main force in hostile territory. Each possess their own mystery, but without cooperation and trust, they will be doomed to failure.

Pressed into Service is the introduction to the bold Pilgrims with Blades series.

Dhea Loral